AFTER THE STORM

BY

ADEGOKE AUSTIN
ADEDAMOLA
TRIPLE A

Published by New Generation Publishing in 2019

First Edition

All the characters in this book have no existence outside the imagination of the author, and have no relationship whatsoever to anyone bearing the name or names. They are not even distantly inspired by any individual known or unknown to the author, and all the incidents are pure invention.

ISBN:

Author's Contact Address.
Federal Ministry of Agriculture And Rural Development, Area 11, Garki, Abuja, Nigeria

E-mail – triplea4you@yahoo.com

Tel.- +234 (0) 8029104044

www.newgeneration-publishing.com

ABOUT THE AUTHOR

Adegoke Austin Adedamola, hails from Ibadan in Oluyole Local Government of Oyo State, attended Ibadan Grammar School (1984-86), Bishop Phillip Academy, (1986-1989), Saint Andrew's College of Education, (1990-1993) and Ahmadu Bello University Zaria (1997-2002). A politically active individual popularly known as TRIPLE A, was a one-time Secretary General of African Union Students Club (OAU), 2000/2001 and Chairman of African Union Students Club A.B.U. Zaria (2001/2002), the Founder and Executive Director of Youth Awareness Movement Against AIDS in Africa (YAMAA) A.B.U Chapter (1999/2002). The Founder and Chairman Implementation Committee of NAVOTEDS, (2001/2002). An Aspirant for the post of Director of Food and Welfare (ABUSUG 2000), a member of Caretaker Committee ABUSUG (2001/2002) and a member of Creative Writers Club A.B.U. Zaria. He holds his B.Sc. (Ed) in Agriculture from Ahmadu Bello University, Zaria, (1997/2002).

A handsome and God fearing gentleman who has practically combine creativity and intellectualism with politics, he has written many short stories, articles and poems published and unpublished.

AFTER THE STORM is a story that centers on man's moral influence on his life and conceitedly indicates all attributes needed to be successful in life. All characters in the book are attributes that play major roles in climbing the ladder of success, which is mostly dominated by WISDOM and UNDERSTANDING.

"Wisdom is the ability of making best use of knowledge, experience and understanding".

– *Late* Rev. (Prof.) Ishaya Audu.

The first indigenous Vice Chancellor of ABU Zaria.

DEDICATION

TO THE ALMIGHTY GOD,
THE CUSTODIAN OF ALL
WISDOM,
KNOWLEDGE AND UNDERSTANDING.

ACKNOWLEDGEMENT

"How much better to get Wisdom than gold, to choose understanding rather than silver!"

All glory and honor belong to God, who in his infinite mercy strengthened me to write. Therefore, I am highly grateful to my heavenly father whose love and inspiration sustained me during the course of writing this book. Despite all odds and difficulties encountered in the process of writing, the Grace of the Lord finally made it possible.

I am particularly indebted to all those who have in one way or the other contributed to the completion of this book. Mention must be made of Mallam. Muazu Maiwada of the Dept. of Literature A.B.U. Zaria, who on his first time of reading the manuscript encouraged me to move on and take time to expand the work, he also assisted me with valuable suggestions that added immeasurably to my logic of writing. Also, Mr. Jegede of the Demonstration Secondary School, who painstakingly read through the manuscript and gave some technical support for a good story book in the field of literature.

Also, I am grateful to Mr. Johnson K. Ayodele the typist who on so many occasions added or removed from the manuscripts as the inspiration directed, to have a complete storybook.

My thanks also goes to my friends and associates particularly *Mr Rowland I Okororie, Miss Joy Campbell* who read the manuscript for their words of encouragement and suggestions before its final publication.

Also, I wish to inform the readers that all names mentioned in the book has nothing to do with individual(s), they are just imaginary names as prompted by the inspirational impetus that directed the writer's mode of writing.

Reference also goes to the author of various quotes used, most especially the author of the book of **Proverbs**, one of my favorite books in the Bible for making it possible for me to select verses that are best suited for the expression of my thought in quotes form. While other quotes are formulated by the author to serve a unique purpose in the book and to make my contribution to the world of numerous quotes in existence.

In conclusion, thanks be to the Lord whose mercies endureth forever and whose divine support has made this dream a reality. (A twenty year challenge)

CHAPTER ONE

"The direction of your vision determines the expression of your mission".

Once upon a time in a small village called Endurance, There was a particular old man called Hope, who had three grown-up children.

The eldest son was called Repercussion; the second, Greediness while the third was named Success. The people of this village were very hardworking and successful in their business endeavors. Success; the youngest son of Hope, was a very humble and hardworking man.

Hope, being a very poor old man of seventy was catered for by his children, who worked hard day and night to provide for the family.

One day, after supper in front of his mud house under a bright full moon that sparingly lit the whole village, Hope called his children and informed them that he wants them to engage in a business of their choice. Then he gave them three shillings each, after which, he asked them of the businesses they would do with the money.

The eldest brother said, he had made up his mind to be a great farmer, while the second said he would like to be a produce buyer. However, to the astonishment of Hope, Success the youngest said, he would use his money to buy wisdom.

All were surprised at Success' saying because they couldn't think of anybody far or near that was selling wisdom. The father asked Success how he intends to buy wisdom, since there was nobody in Endurance selling wisdom.

Success replied he would embark on a journey to neighbouring villages, until he gets somebody that could sell wisdom to him. Hope then blessed them and they all went in to sleep.

Early in the morning, Success embarked on a journey in search of where to buy wisdom. He traveled to far villages and neigbouring town without finding any wisdom seller.

While on the journey with no hope of buying wisdom in sight, he came to a very thick forest, which seemed to him the end of the world. Instead of being discouraged, he summoned courage and entered the forest of Fortune. He vowed not to return home until he had bought wisdom.

He wandered in the Forest for so many months, not minding what might happen to him. He slept in caves, tree shades and many other shelters he could find. Besides fruits, small rodents were his food for months in the Forest of Fortunes.

Then, one cool evening of his last month in the great forest, something very frightening happened. A wild wind suddenly began with very high intensity. All living things in the forest were seriously disturbed, as wild and dangerous animals ran helter-skelter, lions were roaring, elephants trumpeting, snakes hissing, jaguar yowling, reptiles crawling from one place to another.

Thus, there was confusion in Fortune, an ironical forest that often smiles on people. It was a forest of mysteries and wonders; the abode of mysterious beings, the habitat of the fiercest and dangerous animals, the home of unearthly apparitions, the jungle of uncertainty where everything seemed unpredictable. Nevertheless, ***"fortune only favor the prepared minds".***

Success was terribly scared and disturbed in the forest that evening. He had never witnessed this type of mighty storm in his life but suddenly the cloud gathered and the storm turned the day in to night unexpectedly. Meanwhile, the storm had displaced him from his former abode to another. Despite the fact that he held tightly to the branch of a tree, he found himself thrown down flat and terribly terrified.

When Success raised his head he saw an old grey-haired man in white garment, holding a staff and was bare-footed. The toothless old man looked scary and taller than normal with wrinkles all over his face. When he spoke the forest vibrated in submission.

The old man greeted Success and asked him of his mission in the Forest of Fortune where many had entered but few only managed to come out alive. "This is a forest that was full of the unexpected, the unimaginable and the unpredictable" said the old man. Success then explained his mission to the old man with fear and trembling. The old man laughed and the whole forest re-vibrated again and this made Success to be more terrified. He told Success **"I am Understanding, the eldest brother of Wisdom."**

Understanding collected three shillings from **Success** and advised him on three virtues he must always remember to have in life. The first was to always remember to thank anybody that helps him or does him a favour. The second was to always keep secrets, while respect for the elders was the last advise to **Success**. Thereafter, **Understanding** vanished out of sight.

Success was depressed and became more confused because, he could not understand the reason for these three-point admonition to him by the old man. Success, thought they were just a common and simple virtues a decently brought up person would observe always.

Now, he had no idea where to go as he felt the old man had robbed him of his money. Success continued to wander in the forest in despair and lost hope of buying wisdom. He wandered hopelessly for seven days after his encounter with Understanding.

At dawn, Success came to a narrow path in the forest of Fortune, which he followed to nowhere. Success became exhausted and could not move again. He contemplated of killing himself, but he felt, he should rather be eaten up by any wild animals that came around, than for him to go back home without accomplishing his mission in life. It was with this thought that he fell down and slept off not knowing that Fate was not far away from him anymore. It was in this oblivious condition, that he sensed somebody was beside him. Success then regained consciousness. He had never met any human being since his wandering began in the terrible forest of Fortunes.

His guest was a young lady with a pot of water on her head. She was staring at Success with pity. He instantly begged the lady for water to drink and she gave him without hesitation. She didn't utter a word to him and left but Success quickly thanked her for her kind gesture.

The young lady was surprised and she turned back to look at Success more closely. She wondered what he could be doing in the Forest, or perhaps he was a hunter without a gun or may be a wanderer. Success narrated his story and experience in the forest of Fortune to her. She was deeply sorry and then realized Success was a stranger. She therefore decided to help him.

All along, Success did not know where he was until this lady spoke. "I am Love, the only daughter of Favor, who is the king of this village called Fate". Then he realized that he had been talking with a Princess. Love helped Success and led him to Peace, her father's Palace.

People were surprised to see the perceived arrogant Princess with a ragged man. Many suitors both rich and poor, had asked Love's hand in marriage, but she always turned them down. This attitude many considered as pride and disrespect. Love, [being a beautiful gem, with has the ability to hold things together and upon which the existence of a man is built, without which the man's existence becomes questionable],was considered as the builder of every good home and the only Princess of Fate, that can change a worthless substance to a valuable material.

"The fear of the omnipotent is the commencement of wisdom".

The king was worried to see Love, his daughter with a stranger, he was displeased and disappointed seeing his daughter moving around with a stranger in Fate. Love called her father aside and narrated the whole story of the ragged man to him. She felt that, Success might be her husband to-be and she had made up her mind to marry Success.

King Favour was baffled but extremely happy, because, the Princess had long been due for marriage. All attempts to get her a husband among the rich men within and outside the town were in vain.

King Favour ordered one of his servants to take care of Success and adorn him in fine garment and royal accessories. Happiness, the eldest brother of Love was also delighted to see Success. Success was well-fed and beautifully dressed. He looked radiant in his outfit. Favour then called on Success to narrate his story once more. He did without mincing words, how he suffered for many months in the forest of Fortune where he was finally "robbed" of his three shillings by an old man.

Nobody could really comprehend his story, they wondered, how a greenhorn like Success could be in quest of wisdom to buy. Besides what was wisdom?, who was selling it?, how does it look like?, these were many questions that was troubling the mind of the king and his people. The king told him that, wisdom is not on sale in his village but asked Success whether he was prepare to marry his daughter and live with them in Fate. Success agreed to marry Love, the only daughter of Favour and stay with them in Fate. Fate is a mysterious village that lifts someone to the highest pedestal of life and also defeat or condemned others permanently to the pit of life.

CHAPTER TWO

"All noble things are as difficult as they are rare".

The marriage ceremony of Success and Love was very colourful. Eminent people from the neighbouring villages such as Prestige, Honour, and Fame among others came on Favour's invitation to grace the occasion. The guests brought gifts of gold, silver, diamond and many valuable gifts to the new couple. Success was very delighted with the ceremony and decided to settle in Fate, as he was at peace with his new environment.

Success and Happiness, the elder brother of Love struck a friendship and this thrilled Favour the more, as his chiefs also liked him. Success became very close to the king and also lived like a Prince in Fate and they all dwelled together in Peace, the notable name of Favour's palace.

Peace, the palace of Favour contains many queens among whom was Temptation, the most beautiful queen of all Favour's wives. Her beauty made the king to love her the most, but Temptation was of bad character, full of manipulation and very crafty in nature.

Her bad character made people in the palace to avoid her. Sadly, Temptation was not bothered about her behaviour and what people think about her. She continued in her pride and lecherous attitude.

Everyday was like a festival in Peace because of Favour's kindness and generous disposition, assorted foods including bush meat were delicacies in his palace. Faith whom had being a popular butcher in Fate for a long time always come to Fate from Sorrow, a neighbouring town with assorted bush meat to sell to the king. Most times, he delivered the meat to Temptation because she was in charge of the king's food.

The situation had created an avenue for free interaction between her and Faith and their closeness grew secretly.

The latter too, a good-looking man from Sorrow was attracted to Temptation, with her captivating beauty. The seductive power of Temptation, completely engulfed Faith and led to an unholy relationship between them which nobody suspected for a long time in Peace.

"The event of the day determines the condition of a man".

This Temptation's illicit affair with Faith, eventually put the whole Palace into confusion and nearly cost Success his life.

Success one day assumed the responsibility of taking care of the palace whenever Favour the king is not around. Success was saddled with leadership position to supervise everything in Peace before Favour comes back. This accorded Success the opportunity to exercise his leadership potentials in the Palace. He was very conscious of the trust and confidence the king had reposed in him and was prepared not to let him down. He believed that, ***"responsibility without ability is always a calamity".*** Therefore, he was ready to go extra miles in discharging the duties assigned to him by the king.

He therefore employed his creative talent which was inherent in all creatures but only few exhibits this potentials. These qualities, which only few individuals recognize; are commitment, sincerity of purpose, sense of direction, good judgment, focus, absolute concentration and ability to go extra-miles in resolving problems, all these qualities were carefully employed by Success in discharging his duties in the kings' palace. With all these, Love supported him. He was able to turn things around extraordinarily in Fate before the King came back. Success believed that ***"the efficacy of a man is not in his despondency but in his bouncy".***

Happiness, the eldest son of Favour along side some important chiefs had also accompanied the king on his journey. The exemplary leadership of Success made him to be in charge of Peace and he took charge of Peace with absolute sense of maturity. Favour's mind was always at rest, once Success is in-charge.

One eventful evening, as Success was carrying out his daily routine round the Palace, he met Faith and Temptation coming out of the latter's room in a suspicious manner. Temptation was ashamed to encounter Success in her shameful condition. Success, whom apart from Favour and his children had the authority to enter the queen's harem was dumbfounded to see this shameful act committed by these two people against the King.

Success was in a confused state as Temptation and Faith pleaded in tears for Success to keep their secret. He was deeply touched by their crime and since he knew the punishment for their crime is public hanging, he then promised to keep their secret from his majesty only if they also promise to desist from such obnoxious act against the king. Success didn't know that, the deed had been done.

It wasn't long after this incident that the king returned from his pilgrimage, but things had gone sour in Peace.

The physical condition of Temptation was very obvious to everybody in the palace and there were silent murmuring going round in Peace.

The matter was finally exposed when the bewildered King arrived and saw the condition of his beloved wife.

Favour was furious and greatly disturbed by the shameful condition he met his wife. It was obvious to most people that nobody should be responsible for this act than Success, as he was the only person with the right to enter the harem. Other queens had also testified they had been seeing Success in the harem during his supervision as he used to exchange pleasantries with them to know their needs and conditions.

Love and Happiness felt bad over this matter but were convinced that Success could not have done this outrageous crime to the king that loved him dearly. Nevertheless, the whole situation was still cloudy and complex to comprehend, more so, Temptation deliberately turned the whole story against Success by lying that Success had impregnated her. She was surprisingly supported by Sin, her immediate step-wife, who had been receiving various gifts from her for so long, meanwhile, Temptation and Sin are also the only identical twin in Fate from Wickedness who is also the mother of Evil.

CHAPTER THREE

"The integrity of the uprights will guide them, but the perversity of the unfaithful will destroy them".

Success was shocked because there was nothing he could do or say to save his life. More so that he had vowed not to reveal the secret of the affair between Temptation and Faith. Besides, he had no witness to back him up like Temptation, who had the support of Sin, her immediate step wife, whom Temptation had bribed. However, Charity their eldest wife was indifferent, even though she had caught Faith on one or two occasions coming out of Temptation's room in a suspicious manner.

Charity saw no reason to back Success up, since she could not convince Favour at that moment. But she believed that Success was innocent. Similarly, Destiny, the Father of Prosperity and Poverty, a strange old man in Fate knew Success was innocent. Destiny was considered to have an unrevealed unrivaled power from the Creator to gain control over man's life, he too was grieved over the fate of Success but prayed passionately for his vindication.

There was much consultation, deliberation and discussion between Favour and his noble chiefs. They resolved to use the traditional means to solve the matter following the plea by Success that he was not responsible for the pregnancy of the queen, and therefore insist he was not guilty.

To resolve any cloudy matter in Fate, Success would be sent to Sorrow, a small town where Failure was their king with the traditional message that would prove his innocence. The message contained a small quantity of fresh soil, wrapped with a fresh leaf, all inside a small fresh calabash with a two-edged sharp sword all sealed in a well-decorated box.

It was very difficult for someone to come back alive from Sorrow except one meets Mercy, the compassionate goddess that dwells in the Forest of Struggle on his way to Sorrow.

Many, such as Lust, the eldest brother of Infatuation, Covetousness and Anger have passed through this Forest of Struggle without returning.

The Forest of Struggle often referred to by men as Wilderness of Life was a dreadful one, with lots of tribulations, humiliations, victimizations, disappointments and afflictions. To be sent on errand through the forest of Struggle was a test to confirm the innocence of an individual over difficult matters not clear in Fate.

The king was so grieved over the assignment given to his beloved in-law and diligent servant to Sorrow. Nevertheless, the tradition must be observed, for the law of the land in Fate is one which no one has control over and this law knows no one. Love became sick and emaciated, she refused to eat, all persuasions and advice to pacify her failed. In the early hours of the morning, Success was sent out of Fate, amidst many sympathizers crying.

Success had summoned the courage with a strong conviction that he was innocent and was not bothered or worried about the whole problem which fate could not resolve, he believed he was only conveying a fine box to Sorrow, the implication or the danger of which was not clear to him.

“Determination is the soul of Success”

Prior to Success' departure, he had assured his wife of his innocence and had a similar talks with Happiness and Comfort, his wife childhood friend who had earlier cheered him and they all wished Success well on his journey to Sorrow.

On getting to the boundary between Fate and the Forest of Struggle to Sorrow. His sympathizers departed and he proceeded on his journey to the land of Sorrow. Success remembered his former days in the Forest of Fortune which made him not to be intimidated by the terrible Wilderness of Life, the wilderness that is full of unforeseen forces, unimaginable circumstances, predicaments and challenges, the Forest of struggle where many things becomes unpredictable, the Wilderness of life, where there is no absolute finish line for anybody, it is a place where men have different tracks with different durations, where the only thing that is common to men is the empire of life itself, it is only few that can pass through the wilderness of life unharmed, a place where someone may struggle to become successful at an early age but die sooner than expected while others take longer time to make it in the wilderness of life but live longer than expected. A place where many get married as a virgin but have to wait a decade or more to conceive and be blessed with children, while another after series of abortion in her past becomes a mother almost immediately after marriage, the Wilderness of life that is full of irony in itself.

Success had barely covered a long distance when he became tired and wish to sit down to rest under the Tree of Procrastination, a young man suddenly appeared from nowhere, he told Success that he was sent by Mercy, the goddess of the wilderness of life and his name is Courage. Courage, encouraged Success not to rest or relax, but to continue his journey with a promise to lead him to his destination because to sit or rest was forbidden in this Forest of Life.

Success thanked Courage and they set out together in this terrible Forest, as soon as they got to the Mountain of Discouragement, the Mountain that was rough, slippery and taller than normal, Success had never seen this type of Mountain in his life as they spent several days to climb and descend to the other side of the mountain. The Mountain of Discouragement in the Forest of Struggle is one of the natural obstacles to overcome by many men passing through the Wilderness of life and failure to do this may result in a terrible un-accomplishment. While many people had gotten to this place and lost their lives others had managed to descend but failed to proceed further due to lack of direction and divine vision.

Success and Courage were able to climb and descend this Mountain Successfully. It was on this Mountain Anger died and Revenge lost his life. While moving ahead Success became exhausted and worn-out but Courage supported him as the land of Sorrow was still far away. Courage told Success that on the Mountain of Discouragement, ***"quitters never wins and winners never quit".***

The second hurdle in the Forest of Struggle, was the River of Setback. At this point fatigue and despondence set in, Success wanted to turn back, especially when he was confronted by the six wicked sisters that dwelled in the River of Setback. The wicked sisters ganged up against Success due to the enviable reports they used to receive from Sin their fellow sister who married to Favour, the King of Fate about Success.

It was Sickness that first attacked Success on his way to Sorrow, surprisingly Suffering also joined issues with Success, before Success could come out of their attack, Stagnancy held Success down for a longtime in the River of Setback, it was in the process of Success coming out from the grip of Stagnancy that Shame appeared.

Shame who humiliated Success in this river was not afraid to hide her feelings about Success. She told Success that it was impossible for any man to pass through the River of Setback without been hurt by the six wicked sisters, as it was the tradition of the River of Setback to destroy every good intentions of man, take away man's vision and bewitch man's mind with death.

Also that, it was only Sin that was lucky to get married out of the six sisters, as no man desired to have any affairs or relationship with sickness, suffering, stagnancy, shame and suicide, this made them to be dangerous and hazardous to human existences and they afflict men without mercy anytime they have opportunity to vent their frustration with anyone that crosses their path.

The matter became worse for Success when the last of this wicked sister, Suicide appeared, She afflicted Success' mind immediately to kill himself. She told Success that the River of Setback is a terrible river, full of negative thoughts, unholy intentions and irrational behaviors, unguided utterances, where the thoughts of men became shallow and fascinated toward death. She told Success that there is no hope for him again in life.

Suicide told him that Success can only be delivered by Boldness as Courage is not enough to overcome the six sisters that dwells in the River of Setback.

Success reflected on various difficulties he had on his way, he summoned Boldness for assistance and crossed this difficult River of Setback victoriously to move ahead. Boldness told Success that, this dreadful river had drown Covetousness and Hatred long ago, in the river of setback, you must never be weary to move ahead as the river has its funny way of dragging men behind to lose their missions in life. Boldness told Success that, in the River of Setback, Fornication, Prostitution, Masturbation and Adultery were the major instruments of attraction for destruction in this river.

Success' journey began proper after successfully crossing the River of Setback, Courage left him as Boldness appeared to take over, Boldness a wealthy businessman is used to crossing the River of Setback without any assistance and fortunately for Success, Boldness was on his way to Mistake, Sorrow's market, the market where people always trade garments of agony, pains, disappointment, boredom and different kind of crimes.

The thought of getting to Sorrow had occupied Success' mind and he asked Boldness the location of Sorrow's town. He replied that Sorrow was a small town at the other side of the Valley of Reality, ***but only few people can see Reality of life in the forest of struggle since it is always elusive in most men's mind.***

CHAPTER FOUR

The two had a long rest based on the advice of Boldness that they must try and crossover the Valley of Reality in the day time, because the Valley of Reality is where everything becomes original and pure, a valley where there is no illusion and where thoughts and imaginations strengthen the vision of men and truth becomes absolute ingredients to succeed in life. Also, it was a saying in the valley of reality '**that ye shall know the truth and the truth shall set you free**'. Moreover, ***It is a fact that in the Forest of Struggle, there is only one true way to reality because the other ways lead to perdition and the short cut is perilous.***

Therefore, Success and Boldness successfully crossed the Valley of Reality unhurt which was the Valley where Pride, Envy and Lust had lost their lives and Strife had also perished. Now, It dawned on Success that Courage had long gone and Boldness had been in-charge. This made him come to conclusion that man needs more than Courage to face the reality of life.

Eleven months had passed since Success had been on his journey through the Wilderness of life, Success eventually reached Sorrow successfully. He was so happy that he was able to fulfill his mission and his goal of delivering his king's message, he believed that ***"a man without a goal in the wilderness of life is a goat".*** Meanwhile, he had no idea the location of the King's Palace, as he was a complete stranger in the Land of Sorrow; the land that was full of bitterness, tragedies, disasters, wars and recurring crimes.

As he was passing through "Mistake" the popular market in sorrow, he accidentally met Faith, who was very glad to see Success but wondered what his mission could be in the land of Sorrow, since the people of Fate had nothing in common with the people of Sorrow.

Success told him that he had a message from Favour, the King of Fate for Failure, the King of Sorrow. Faith looked at the beautiful box in the hand of Success suspiciously, but had no idea of what its content was, since nobody could guess the nature of the message from Favour to Failure until it was revealed. Beside, messages between the two had always been secretive, both Kings have been exchanging messages with each other for many years. However it was noticed that anybody sent from Failure to Favour always refuse to come back to Sorrow, because Favour generally bless them and makes their lives better, but reverse is the case with Failure, he was known as the owner of affliction, tribulation and lamentation, therefore, it was very difficult to know the nature of message from Favour to Failure since not all the people sent to Failure do come back alive.

Faith thanked Success for saving his life from Favour by not revealing his relationship with Temptation. Success told him that all was well in Fate. Faith persuaded Success to follow him to his house to take some rest before seeing the King since Success was tired and hungry.

Faith took great care of Success and volunteered to take the box to the King of Sorrow the next day. Success agreed since he believed that, ***"one good turn deserves another"***, but forgetting that, ***"the evil men do lives after them"***. *Faith*, woke up very early in the morning and took the message to Confusion; Failure's Palace.

CHAPTER FIVE

"Evil pursue sinners, but to the righteous, good shall be repaid'

Failure was a very hostile King of Sorrow. He had no regard for anybody, hence, ruled the land of Sorrow in collaboration with all his Chiefs as a tyrant. Among his Chiefs were Frustration, Rejection, Depression and Hopelessness to mention but a few, they all prevailed in Sorrow. His wife Poverty was not also a kind woman at all, she was regarded as the witch of Sorrow who killed the Conscience of men. These people made the kingdom of sorrow a land that was full of weeping and gnashing of teeth. The spouse live in Confusion, a notable name for Failure's Palace.

Failure received Favour's message with care and handed it over to Hopelessness one of his chiefs as the tradition demands in Sorrow, It was Depression that will then divulge the content of the message to the king.

Immediately, the message was deciphered, Faith was called in and he was beheaded by stern-looking Frustration, the chief executioner to Failure. They put Faith's fresh head in a calabash and it was securely placed in a well sealed box.

The execution was done according to the message from Favour which reads ***"this man had committed a crime in our land – behead him."*** Failure's messenger, Laziness would then carry the message back to Favour, if there is nobody from Fate to carry the box.

"The righteousness of the blameless will direct his way aright, but the wicked will fall by his own wickedness".

Success, did not know what had taken place in the Palace. He was waiting impatiently for his friend to return to deliver the outcome of the message. When he couldn't withstand it any more, he rose and went to Confusion,

Failure's Palace not knowing that it was ***"by Grace he was saved through Faith."***

On getting to the palace, he was quickly recognized by Failure as a stranger. Success was asked where he came from, he told Failure he was from Fate. Failure ordered Rejection, one of his chiefs to hand over the box to Success without further interrogation because his appearance to Failure was intimidating, as Failure could not withstand Success' appearance. Therefore, he was unceremoniously ushered out of Confusion by Hopelessness, who guided him through Victory route back to Fate.

Success was busy gazing at one ugly man that sat at a corner of Confusion, the man became irritated and shouted at him "why are you staring at me like a fool? Don't you know that I'm Hardship, the only son of Failure and Poverty and the only Prince of Sorrow?" Success became frightened but remained calm.

He did not know that nobody dare look Hardship in the face in the land of Sorrow, a terrible Prince that terrified both old and young.

Success couldn't understand the reason behind the urgency with which he was ushered out of Confusion with such hostility. He became more worried due to the face of Hardship, the son of Poverty that was horrible and tormenting.

But, he was satisfied with his box on his way back to Fate. Success realized the box was a bit heavier than before. Success kept going without looking back so as not to see the horrible faces of Failure, Poverty, Hardship and their cruel chiefs again.

During the course of his Journey, Success was worried and disturbed for not being allowed to thank Faith who had helped him deliver his message.

The tradition in Fate was that after twelve months, Favour would send Confidence, one of his noble chiefs, to collect the message from Sorrow after the message had been delivered. Confidence sighted Success on Victory route which is a sacred route for any ordinary man to trek except those that had been saved from Failure's hands and escaped the horror of Sorrow. Confidence on sighting Success, became afraid and ran back to Fate, with the thought that he had seen Success' ghost coming back to Fate.

Confidence was panting and sweating profusely while telling the King and his Chiefs that he saw the ghost of Success coming with the King's box to the Palace. Favour was scared and all the chiefs were afraid because, the King must not see a ghost,

They thought that Success must have been killed by Failure or his spirit was wandering because of his passion for Love, Happiness and the good people of Peace. They believed his ghost was coming back to haunt the Palace.

CHAPTER SIX

The just shall live by faith"

There was pandemonium and confusion in Peace when success finally arrived. All the magicians were ordered to send the ghost back but to no avail, it was later comfirmed that success was real. The King came out with exceedingly great joy from his inner chamber where he had been hidden to receive Success.

Happiness and Love were overwhelmed with joy. Success innocence has now been established by his arrival, for few people such as Truth and Belief had gone to Sorrow and came back alive. Nevertheless, there was an outburst of jubilation amidst surprise when the King's box was finally opened in the public.

Success nearly ran mad when he saw Faith's head in the box. Then it became clearer to him that the content of the King's box was for him to be killed, as it was a common prayer in Fate that ***"may you never carry the King's box"*** the meaning of which he bothered not to know since he had been living in Fate. Success was to be beheaded on the belief that he had an affair with the king's wife. Now, the truth had prevailed and justice had been served to the perpetrator.

Success then recalled the prayers of Destiny a strange old man, the Father of Prosperity and Poverty who dwell in Fate. He concluded that it was Destiny's prayer that guided him out of Failure's hand for he consulted Destiny before his departure to the land of Sorrow, a practice which people seldom do. Success was then convinced that ***"nemesis catches up with all evildoers no matter how long".***

The King and his chiefs were astonished to see the head of Faith in the box because he was the popular King's butcher. The people could not really comprehend the mystery of finding the head of Faith in the King's box, though it had been long he came to Peace.

Success then beckoned his majesty to call his wife, Temptation who had just given birth to a bouncing baby girl called Deceit, to see what was in the calabash. She emerged full of arrogance that soon melted away. On seeing the head of Faith inside the calabash, Temptation became unconscious and collapsed immediately.

This Palace drama of Faith's-head-in-King's-box was interesting but riddled with confusion as nobody understood the unfolding scenario and none could readily linked the death of Faith to Temptation, the wife of their king. The Life Oracle as Destiny is usually called, was consulted to reveal and interpret the meaning of a particular event in the town that seems to pose a riddle to the king and his chiefs. Destiny, a very popular man, that holds information about the present and future of man which man has no control over, revealed to the people of Fate that, at times men's faith needed to be stronger, because not every person can resist the power of Temptation in most situations. He added that the real Faith he knows ***is the substance of things people hope for and the evidence of things not seen by men.*** The People could not understand the interpretation given by Destiny on Faith.

To clear the situation, Success finally spoke. He narrated the whole story to the King and his chiefs. The narration of Success was then surprisingly confirmed by Charity who declared that in some instances she had also caught them in the act. Temptation could not deny the stories of her affairs with Faith. It then became very clear to Favour, his chiefs, and the people of Fate that the mischief of Temptation which initially implicated Success, his trial and vindication eventually proved him innocent. The news spread like wild fire all over the town that Success the man people loved and wrongly implicated to die, had returned alive from Sorrow with the head of Faith.

This made his personality, integrity and credibility became enhanced and strengthened in Fate and its environs.

His majesty Favour, the King of Fate, was deeply touched by the disgusting event in the Palace. Therefore, he commanded that Temptation, his beloved and dear wife be hanged in public.

Many people jubilated, because the truth had finally prevailed and justice was done. It was also clear to people that, ***"when it goes well with the righteous, the city rejoice and when the wicked perish, there is jubilation".***

Sin the step-wife of Temptation, who collaborated with her to bear false witness against Success realized that she could not exist without Temptation in the Palace and fled from Peace with Deceit, Temptation's daughter.

The People of Fate now realized that it was possible for Temptation to kill Faith and also determine the existence of Sin. They finally concluded that where there is no Temptation, Sin cannot live but where Temptation overpowers Faith, Sin rejoices. Unfortunately for Sin, nobody had ever had any commitment to Sin in Fate, therefore Sin's disappearance was not felt or noticed by the good people of Fate.

As for the young Deceit, people were glad that Sin took her away. They believed that a cub would always resemble the Lion, invariably meaning Deceit will surely behave like her mother as she was also captivatingly beautiful and secondly, Favour, the King does not like Deceit at all.

Harmony was finally brought back to Peace, when Happiness, Love and Success saw each other. Ever since, they continued living together in Peace, the beautiful Palace of Favour, the King of Fate. ***"Though they joined forces, the wicked will not go unpunished, but the posterity of the righteous will be delivered"***, Destiny the oldest man of Fate who had been following the trend of events in the town with all sincerity concluded.

CHAPTER SEVEN

After many years of staying in Fate, Success became home sick and desired to go back to his town. He didn't know how to reveal his feelings to the king as he was very conscious of Favour's Love for him; hence he did not want to hurt the king's feelings.

Success became nervous in attempt to hide his feelings. Success then called Love his wife to seek her opinion on this matter. He thought that Love would not understand or support his wish to leave Fate. Success was astonished because Love was more fascinated with the news of going to her husband's town after many years they had been leaving together in Fate. Comfort who is a friend of Love came to plead with the king of Fate on their behalf to allow them go back to Endurance.

But Happiness was not too pleased initially that Success was about to leave their town, nevertheless, following pleadings from Success, Love and Comfort, Happiness agreed to plead with Favour to approve the departure of Success from Fate to Endurance.

Favour was caught unaware by this news but he was a bit comfortable when he saw Comfort his daughter's childhood friend with them as she is somebody Favour did not want to hurt or discomfort in anyway, he then ponder seriously on this great development.

His majesty, Favour could not come to terms on the possible departure of Success because he exhibited some characters and qualities, besides, Favour knew that Success is a man of uncommon abilities and indefatigable industries, these were quite distinct and very uncommon in an ordinary human being and also that Success was imbibed with dedication, punctuality, honesty, obedience, diligence, kindness, to mention but a few. As all these qualities were considered to be attributes of a successful man.

However, after seven days he gladly gave his consent to release Success to go home and promised to remember him for unforgettable things he had accomplished in Fate. Favour then blessed Success with wonderful gifts including half of his possessions.

The gifts were horses, slaves, money, gold, silver, diamonds, bronze, garments, jewelries and many other valuable items which were not common in those days. Thus, Success became a rich and honourable man in Fate.

On the third day to his departure from Fate, there was great celebration in the town of Fate, this event was graced by distinguished persons and eminent personalities such as Prosperity, Prestige, Reward, Justice, Fame and Honour to mention a few, who came from neighbouring towns on the invitation of Favour

Failure the King of Sorrow, his wife Poverty, their only child Hardship and their chiefs, Frustration, Depression, Hopelessness and Rejection couldn't grace this momentous occasion, because they could not withstand the presence of Success and as they considered all people invited by Favour as their enemies since they have nothing in common with these good people. Prosperity, Rewards, Justice, Prestige, Honour and Fame marveled at the king's benevolence on Success and they concluded that ***"Favour is the only flavor that can colour a man's labour"*** *as they all departed after the occasion.*

On the fourth day, many people gathered again for Success' departure. Happiness and Comfort, their closest friends decided to go with them and spend some days in Endurance. Love was happy and she gathered their four children, Hardwork, Satisfaction, Self-denial and Prayer together and they were also happy to follow their father to Endurance.

Amidst joyous mood and praises, Success and his entourage left the people of Fate. Destiny, who adored Success greatly, also gave him his blessing as he was going. ***"After all, home is the resting place of a sojourner, there is no place like home".*** Destiny concluded

CHAPTER EIGHT

"The salvation of the righteous is from the Lord and the posterity of the wicked shall be cut off".

The town of Endurance was seven days journey from Fate through the Gentleness road via Self-control, which passes through the Forest of Humility. As the entourage was about to reach the town, news had spread all over Endurance that Success, the Son of Hope was coming home with great wealth and many slaves.

Hope, a very old man of Ninety could not believe his ears but rejoiced that Success, his son whom people had thought died long ago was coming back home. Hope was filled with joy and expectation to see his son again.

Nevertheless, Repercussion, and Greediness were not happy with the news of their brother's return. Though they were rich and successful in their occupations, they became uneasy with the wealth the people reported Success was coming home with.

Therefore, they conspired to kill Success and inherit his property forgetting that, ***"man proposes but only God disposes".*** On the day of his arrival, it was another great day for Success because he was welcomed with much celebration and jubilation. Success was very pleased to be with his people once again after so many years of absence from home.

Patience, the king of Endurance also sent felicitation message to Hope, one of the oldest and most honorable men in Endurance on his son's arrival. Many people gathered in the compound of Hope for merry making.

People of Endurance were greatly amazed with Success' wealth and the kind of people that followed him from Fate, for they were completely different both physically and in characters. Beside, they exhibited the good qualities all men should possess.

Among them were Comfort, Happiness, Love the wife of Success, Success children- Hard work, Self-denial, Satisfaction and Prayer.

Among Favour's delegates were his noble chiefs, Confidence, Obedience, Destiny and Kindness who escorted Success to Endurance. Hope who was very happy to see Success again and he showered blessings on him and his entourage which further aggravated the bitterness of Success brothers' and they planned fast.

"The upright will dwell in the land, and the blameless will remain in it, but the wicked will be cut off from the earth and unfaithful will be uprooted from it".

Success and his family set to pay homage to Patience, the King of Endurance. The palace of Patience is called "Holiness" by the people of Endurance, it was located in the center of the town, beside the popular market of "knowledge", and the only route that linked Holiness with Hope's compound was Judgment route.

A lot of people had gathered, with great expectation in the market of knowledge with Patience, their King to welcome Success with dancing, amidst eating and drinking. The reception was colourful that people began to wonder why Patience would throw such high reception for Success and his entourage.

Sacrifice, the wife of Patience and the mother of Good and Bad, was admiring Success and his family especially Satisfaction, the only daughter of Success, before the final fatal incident happened.

"The last stroke that breaks the camel's back"

The horses were gorgeously dressed and were ready to convey Success and his people to "Holiness" the Palace of Patience. Surprisingly, Success declined. None of them would ride on the horses except his father and his two brothers to honour them with singing and dancing by their admirers. The suggestion caught the two brothers unawares for they had their own plan from Impatience, the twin brother of Patience, an old evil man of Endurance.

Their evil plan fell like a pack of cards as everybody insisted that, they must ride on horses with their father. They had no option than to comply, contrary to their initial plan. The duo had planned to pass through the long route of "Safety" to "Holiness" the Palace of Patience, because they had planted some evils on Judgment routes.

"The righteous is delivered from trouble and it comes to the wicked instead"

On their way to Holiness which is the popular name of Patience's Palace, Hope was in front followed by Repercussion, Greediness, Success, Love his wife, with their children, Prayer, Self-Denial, Satisfaction and Hardwork, Comfort, Happiness, Confidence, Prosperity and Kindness, other members of Favour's delegation with other well wishers. It was a big surprise when Mercy appeared to join them on their journey to Holiness, as it was not her tradition to grace occasion in Endurance except on a special occasion because she was considered to be an invisible goddess that dwells in the land of Endurance.

As they were approaching the centre of knowledge market, an incredible wild storm began that threw the whole "knowledge" into confusion. This storm was powerful that it caused pandemonium in knowledge market. Many people became apprehensive including his majesty "Patience" and his chiefs, Pleasure of Endurance and Fear of Endurance over the wild storm. ***"for one 's eye not to see evil, it is the collective task of the whole body"***, Fear concluded and he fled from knowledge market immediately.

CHAPTER NINE

Success who had seen this type of storm before did not entertain any distress, but did not envisage the enormity of this storm at all.

The troublesome storm made two of the horses to be nervous and they started stampeding and galloping wildly but that of Hope stood firm and relaxed.

The two men were lifted from the back of their horses into the air and thrown down in front of Patience the open-minded king of Endurance with some objects placed on their chest by an invisible hands.

Repercussion died instantly while Greediness was seriously injured and half-conscious. The people gathered round them, while Success held Greediness, his brother close to his chest. Greediness, half conscious, narrated their entire ordeal and revealed to his brother Success that all that had happen was a consequence of their plan to kill Success and inherit his properties.

He further confessed that they had buried a charm for him on Judgment route, where he "Success" would have ride his horse, he added that their plan was shattered, when he insisted that they should ride the horses to honour them instead. This was contrary to their plan to pass through Safety route to Holiness. He stated that the plan was designed and engineered by his brother Repercussion, while the charm was prepared and given to them by Impatience, the twin brother of the King of Endurance, Greediness then concluded that, ***"what patience could not give you, impatience cannot give you either, and that Patience is the only ability to wait for God's time without losing His love".*** *He advised all people present at the knowledge market to be Patient in life* and he dropped dead.

Success was greatly shocked and wept bitterly after hearing the evil plan of his two brothers who on the contrary he had planned to honour them in the presence of

Patience and Sacrifice in knowledge market. The spectators still perplexed and confused in the euphoria of this ugly incidence, but suddenly, a large croaky laughter was heard that frightened everybody. A large noise came from a bare footed, gray-haired and toothless old man. He was in white garment with old staff for support and was wearing a long gray beard begging for attention not to impede his walking.

The old man is called Understanding, the eldest brother of Wisdom. Then he came to a halt and stood in the center of Knowledge Market, in front of the King of Endurance and faced Success. Success quickly recognized him.

Every body was in absolute silence as Understanding spoke saying "***Happy is the man who finds wisdom and the man who gains understanding for her proceeds are better than the profits of silver and her gain than fine gold. Wisdom is more precious than jewels and nothing you desire can compare with her. Long life in her right hand, in her left hand was riches and honour.*** "Success" you are a wise man, for no one can buy wisdom except the Lord giveth. Therefore, cry no more for you have overcome your enemies and you are an upright man in the sight of God and your people". Then with a sharp smile from a toothless mouth, Understanding walked toward Success and finally returned the three shillings collected from him during their previous encounter in the Forest of Fortune twenty years ago.

It was on this note that it dawned on Success that he was advised by Understanding in the Forest of Fortune to always observe these three attributes of thanksgiving, keeping secrets and respecting elders anywhere he finds himself in life, these three attributes had helped him to succeed in life. Though, he exhibited the three unconsciously.

A mixed feeling of Joy and Sadness pervaded the Knowledge Market but the result was acceptable to everybody, because " ***the wages of sin is death and the price of wickedness is suffering".*** These were the words of Pleasure a respectable chief of Patience after the whole incident.

Endurance people went home with great wisdom except "Fear" who had ran away from Knowledge before the arrival of Understanding. Therefore, he could not gain from the teaching of Understanding. Destiny who had been following events as they were unfolding was an old man full of life experiences. He concluded that blessed is the man who endures to the end for inside every endurance lies the secrets of achievement and success in life. Holding on to the law of nature which says ***"the patient dog eats the fattest bones"*** He explained further that few people derive pleasure in endurance while others fear to endure and he who fear to endure in life can not inherit the kingdom of wisdom, because ***"the fear of endurance is the beginning of failure", he stated further that life is full of surprises with different messages for different individual. As the lesson of life can only comes through endurance, patience, sacrifice, these are the embodiment of knowledge.***

CHAPTER TEN

"The end is always sweeter than the beginning"

"My son", Understanding continued, "If you receive my word and treasure up my commandments with you, making your ear attentive to wisdom and including your heart to understanding, yes, if you cry out for insight and raise your voice for understanding, if you seek it like silver and search for it as for hidden treasures, then you will understand the fear of the Lord and find the knowledge of God.

For the Lord gives WISDOM and from his mouth comes knowledge and understanding, he stores up sound wisdom for the upright. He is a shield to those who walk in integrity, guarding the paths of justice and preserving the way of his saints then you will understand righteousness, justice and equity.

Every good path for wisdom will come unto your heart and knowledge will be pleasant to your soul, discretion will watch over you, understanding will guard and guide you, delivering you from the way of evil, from men of perverted speech, who forsake the paths of righteousness to walk in the way of darkness, who rejoice in doing wickedness and delight in the perversion of evil, men whose paths are crooked and who are devious in their ways".

After this message to the people of Endurance, Understanding vanished into the thin air.

Many people were touched by the great message of Understanding, who was the eldest brother of Wisdom. They had never heard such knowledgeable talks in Knowledge Market before. The people became happier and enlightened with his message, but Success was more contented in his heart than usual, and the episode leading to the death of his two brothers still bothered him. Nevertheless, the presence of Comfort comforted him.

Patience, the king of Endurance then blessed Success and declared that day as a day of Success in Endurance to honour Success for his outstanding achievement in life.

Not quite long, after the occasion, running to about six months, Patience an old, un-identical twin brother of Impatience and the king of Endurance passed on.

Success the only son of Hope, the husband of Love, the only friend of Happiness and the father of Hard work, Satisfaction, Self denial and Prayer, automatically became the new king of Endurance, after all ***"it is wiser to have a philosopher as a king than to have a king as a philosopher"*** *Destiny concluded.*

On the day of Success coronation by Experience, another old man in Endurance and a king maker in Endurance, Success spoke to the people of Endurance with great sagacity and wisdom on his life history and experience. He explained that his travails in the Forest of Fortune wasn't easy because he nearly died in this terrible forest adding that his victory was due to Love that drew him to Fate, where he met Favour, Happiness, Confidence, kindness and others in Peace.

He stated that the conspiracy of Temptation and Sin sent him to Sorrow, and not until then, he never realized that it was only Courage and Boldness that could make a man trudge through the Wilderness of life triumphantly, as he overcame all the obstacles in the Forest of Struggle. He paused awhile.

Unknowingly, Destiny worked things out for Success through prayers when he unexpectedly came in contact with Faith the original man that committed the crime in Sorrow. Faith took Success message to Failure where he was beheaded by Frustration.

His voyage back to Endurance can only be through the path of Carefulness in the Forest of Humility. He was optimistic of seeing his people again especially his father, Hope, his brothers, Greediness and Repercussion, Patience the King with Sacrifice his wife and their two lovely children, the Good and the Bad. These are two strong qualities in men, that occurs as a result of nature and are created by circumstances men find themselves.

Success's arrival in Endurance marked a new chapter in the history of the town. The conspiracy of his two brothers that resulted in their painful death was a punishment and the consequence of their unholy association with Impatience, an old devilish man in Endurance who was the un-identical twin brother of Patience the King.

The People of Endurance knew that Impatience was a bad man in their midst, hence only few people consults Impatience for advice, as many understand that any advice from Impatience will always back fire and make men regret for the rest of their life. The dramatic events in Endurance brought Success to the limelight and clothed him with prosperity and victory as he triumphantly overcame his unknown enemies, who had forgotten that ***"greater haste can lead to greater wastes".***

Success then discovered that, Mercy was very essential in overcoming the evil plans of men in all situations, ***"for the fear of the Lord is wisdom and to depart from evil is understanding",.***

Furthermore, while Patience and Sacrifice are the main attributes of living successfully in Endurance, the end result of man's endurance can only be good or bad depending on his destiny, which are usually the unknown circumstances in the life of men and are situation beyond his immediate control that must be fulfilled.

It is of note that those three attributes stated by Understanding yielded positive results in Success' life. He further reechoed the words of kings' friends that, "***in the wildernesses of life Favour is the only flavor that can colour a man's labour'***. In realization of all these, Success, the King of Endurance concluded that ***"In the Wilderness of life, Success is never final, Failure is never fatal, Wisdom, Understanding, Experience with Mercy are some of the vital ingredients needed to sail through the Wilderness of life"*** .

After six months, It was time for Comfort, Happiness and Favour's chief to leave the town, but they felt like staying in Endurance with Success

When the people of Endurance heard of their imminent departure they decided to hold them back by building an edifice each for them in Endurance in appreciation of their contributions and presence in Success' life, this moves they believe will create a sense of belonging for them in Endurance. Actually nobody wanted these good people to leave their town and many people struggle to have them visit their homes before departing from Endurance.

Happiness responded to their kind gesture and told the people that, they had to go but would always be coming to Endurance whenever their attention is needed. They left the town with great joy and happiness," ***the only essence of life which many people are searching for but only few people have them in abundance.***

(Non Scholae sed Vitae.)
Not for School but for Life.

THE END

Watch out
No Man's Business.

www.ingramcontent.com/pod-product-compliance
Ingram Content Group UK Ltd.
Pitfield, Milton Keynes, MK11 3LW, UK
UKHW042001190726
13854UKWH00005B/2105

9 781789 556605